P.B. BEAR

The Marching Band

Lee Davis

FAMILY LEARNING

One sunny day, P.B. Bear and his friend Dermott
were playing in the garden.
RAT-A-TAT-TAT! RAT-A-TAT-TAT!
P.B. Bear banged on his drum.
TOOT! TOOT! TOOT! TOOT!
Dermott blew on his horn.
Back and forth across the garden they marched.
"This is fun!" laughed Dermott.
"We have our very own marching band!"
"Yes!" said P.B. Bear. "Let's find more friends to join us."
So with a RAT-A-TAT-TAT! and a TOOT! TOOT!
they marched through the gate and down the path.

TOOT! TOOT!

RAT-A-TAT-TAT!

They hadn't gone far when they saw
their friend Milly perched up in a tree.
"Hello, P.B.! Hello, Dermott!" called Milly.
"Come and join our marching band!" said P.B. Bear.
"That sounds fun," cried Milly, scurrying down the tree.
She raced home and came back with a tambourine.
"Look! I can make music now," she said.

JINGLE, JANGLE! JINGLE, JANGLE!
Milly shook her tambourine.
So with a **RAT-A-TAT-TAT!** ,
a **TOOT! TOOT!** ,
and a **JINGLE, JANGLE!**
the marching band
carried on down the path.

**JINGLE,
JANGLE!**

Soon the marching band came to a big blue shed.
Their friend Roscoe came out of the shed, eating a carrot.
"What's all that noise?" he asked.
"It's our marching band," said P.B. Bear.
"Would you like to join us?"
"Yes, please!" cried Roscoe.
"I can use my carrot."
"What kind of music does
a carrot make?" asked Dermott.
"Listen," said Roscoe.

CRUNCH, CRUNCH, CRUNCH went Roscoe's carrot.
"It isn't very loud," said P.B. Bear.
"Listen harder," said Roscoe. So they all listened closely.

Roscoe munched and crunched until the carrot was nearly all gone. "Oh, no," he said. "I won't be able to make any sounds when I've finished my carrot, will I? I guess carrots are for eating, not for making music . . ."

CRUNCH!

"So what shall I play?" he asked, going back inside the shed. Soon, he came out with a big bouncy ball. "Listen to this!" he said, bouncing it BOING! BOING! on the path. "I think balls are for bouncing, not for making music," Dermott told him.

BOING!

Next Roscoe got some building blocks from the shed.
He built a very tall tower and knocked it over. **CRASH!**
"I think blocks are for
building, not for
making music,"
Milly told him.
"But I want to be in
your marching band,"
said Roscoe sadly.

CRASH!

"I've got an idea!" cried P.B. Bear.
"Wait for me. I'll be right back!"

P.B. Bear ran home as fast as he could. He went into the kitchen and opened a cupboard.

CLANG! SMASH!

CRASH! CLANG!

"Just what I was looking for!" he cried, pulling out two saucepan lids. Then he ran back to his friends.

"Here you are," said P.B. Bear, giving Roscoe the saucepan lids. "Clap them together like cymbals." Roscoe tried them out. CLANG! CLANG! "Hooray!" cried P.B. Bear. "That's just what we need for our marching band."

CLANG!

CLANG!

The marching band was about to set off when they heard
QUACK! It was their friend Bob.
"Wait for me!" he called.
"Can I join in? I've got
just the thing for a band
leader – a baton!"
"Does a baton make
music?" asked Dermott.
"No," said Bob,
"but I can twirl it.
Watch, everyone!"
Bob tossed the baton
high in the air, **WHIRL**!

Then he caught it *SMACK!* in his bill. The friends gave a loud cheer.

SMACK!

"Come on everyone!"
called Bob.
"Let's march!"

JINGLE, JANGLE!

TOOT! TOOT!

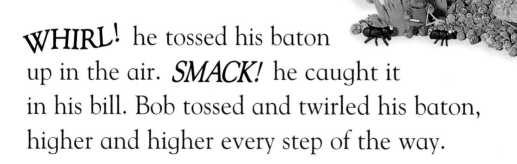

WHIRL! he tossed his baton
up in the air. *SMACK!* he caught it
in his bill. Bob tossed and twirled his baton,
higher and higher every step of the way.

Then, suddenly, Bob missed his baton.
It landed with a great big **THUMP!** right on his foot.
"Ow!" cried Bob in surprise.
He stopped marching . . .

CLANG!

THUMP!

. . . but his friends didn't see him stop!
BOOM*!* P.B. Bear's drum flew into the air.
CLANG! One of Roscoe's cymbals
clattered onto the path. **TOOT!**
Dermott skidded to a stop.
JINGLE! Milly landed
in a heap on top of him.

JINGLE!

TOOT!

QUACK! "What a mess!" Bob squawked.
"Oh dear!" giggled P.B. Bear.
"Can you still march home, Bob?"
"Yes," laughed Bob. "But this time
I think I'll just carry my baton."

BOOM!

QUACK!   CLANG!

Patsy Roscoe P.B. Bear Milly

Bob Hilda Dermott Dixie Russell Florrie

FAMILY LEARNING

Managing Art Editor Chris Fraser **Managing Editor** Bridget Gibbs **Senior Designer** Claire Jones
Senior Editor Caryn Jenner **Project Editor** Natascha Biebow **Designer** Lisa Hollis
DTP Design Kim Browne **Production** Katy Holmes **Photography** Dave King

First published in Great Britain in 1998
Visit us on the World Wide Web at: http://www.dk.com

A CIP catalogue record for this book is available from the British Library.

ISBN 0 7513 7151 3

Reproduced in Italy by G.R.B. Editrice, Verona   Printed and bound in Italy by L.E.G.O.

Acknowledgments
Dorling Kindersley would like to thank the following manufacturers for permission
to photograph copyright material: Ty Inc. for "Toffee" the dog.

Dorling Kindersley would also like to thank Maggie Haden, Richard Blakey, Barbara Owen,
Vera Jones, and Dave King for their help with props and set design.

Can you find me
in each scene?